High and Dry

High and Dry

Eric Walters

Illustrated by
Sabrina Gendron

ORCA BOOK PUBLISHERS

Library and Archives Canada Cataloguing in Publication

Title: High and dry / Eric Walters ; illustrated by Sabrina Gendron.
Names: Walters, Eric, 1957– author. | Gendron, Sabrina, illustrator.
Series: Orca echoes.
Description: Series statement: Orca echoes

Identifiers: Canadiana (print) 20190168935 | Canadiana (ebook) 20190168943 |
ISBN 9781459823105 (softcover) | ISBN 9781459823112 (PDF) | ISBN 9781459823129 (EPUB)
Classification: LCC PS8595.A598 H54 2020 | DDC jC813/.54—dc23

Library of Congress Control Number: 2019943969
Simultaneously published in Canada and the United States in 2020

*Orca Book Publishers is committed to reducing the consumption of nonrenewable resources in the
making of our books. We make every effort to use materials that support a sustainable future.*

Summary: In this illustrated early chapter book, a young boy and
his grandfather work together to save a beached orca.

Orca Book Publishers gratefully acknowledges the support for its publishing
programs provided by the following agencies: the Government of Canada,
the Canada Council for the Arts and the Province of British Columbia
through the BC Arts Council and the Book Publishing Tax Credit.

Cover artwork and interior illustrations by Sabrina Gendron
Author photo by Sofia Kinachtchouk

ORCA BOOK PUBLISHERS
orcabook.com

Printed and bound in Canada.

23 22 21 20 • 4 3 2 1

For Quinn, Isaac and Reese.
—EW

Chapter One

They stood on the dock, looking out at the ocean. The water was dark, with whitecaps, and there were even darker clouds in the sky. The winds were so strong that Dylan felt like they'd be blown away. Looking up, he could see an eagle being pushed along by the wind. Rather than soaring, it looked like it was fighting to get back to the shore.

Dylan could feel spray on his face from the waves crashing on the rocks.

"Isn't it stunning?" his father said.

"What an incredible painting this would be!" his mother exclaimed.

"I'll try to capture it for you so you can paint it later."

His father pulled out one of his ever-present cameras and began taking pictures.

Dylan's dad was a nature photographer, and his mother was a landscape painter. The three of them had lived on this little island for over ten months now, while his parents painted and took photographs. It was beautiful and wild and isolated. For them this had been a paradise to capture and recreate in photographs and paintings.

Dylan loved being with his parents, and he loved their island home, but he

found it a little lonely. It had been better in the summer, when there were other people on the island, living in their vacation homes. But through the winter months Dylan and his parents had been almost all alone, except for a few short visits from family and friends or the occasional summertime family checking on their property.

Dylan was being homeschooled by his parents. Instead of going to school with other children, he did most of his lessons at the kitchen table. He liked that the lessons were different from those he'd had at his regular school, but he missed having other kids around. He missed recess. He missed gym class. He was looking forward to people coming back in the summer. It would be nice to have kids to play with again.

"It's hard to believe our time is almost up," his father said.

"We still have more than four months," his mother answered.

At the end of the summer still to come, they'd go back to their house on the mainland, and Dylan would go back to school. It made him happy thinking about going home to their house, his school and his old friends. He was looking forward to all of that, but he would miss their island home too. He'd miss spending so much time with his parents. He'd miss sitting by the fireplace at night and reading. He'd miss their walks through the woods. Most of all, he'd miss living by the ocean. He loved walking along the beach with his parents and watching the water. And even when he couldn't see it, he could always hear it.

"The waves are *so* high today," Dylan said.

"It's pretty rough," his mother agreed.

"It looks like there's a storm blowing in," his father added.

"Let's just hope it doesn't happen too soon and that the waves aren't too high for the supply ship to dock," his mother said.

"And for Dylan's grandfather to get in," his father said.

That was really what Dylan was thinking about. His mother's father was coming on that boat. He was going to spend the rest of the spring and summer with them. After all, this was Grandpa's home. He'd lived here as a boy, and he came back every summer.

"Do you see them?" his mother asked, pointing.

"Is it the boat?" Dylan asked.

"No, it's the pod," his mother said.

His eyes followed her arm.

"I see them!" Dylan exclaimed.

The dorsal fins of three or four orcas broke the surface. Seeing them made Dylan smile. There were eleven whales in the group that lived in the waters around the island. The group was called a resident pod. He loved seeing the pod. The orcas fed on salmon and often used the cove to trap schools of fish. There were eight adults, two "teenagers" and one younger orca in the group. His father had taken so many pictures of them that when the orcas were close enough, Dylan could tell them apart by their dorsal fins. He and his parents had given them names and gotten to know them. Dylan had called the little one Oreo because both the whale and Dylan's favorite cookie were black and white. They could tell Oreo was a boy by his dorsal fin, which was more triangular in shape.

Dylan and his parents hadn't seen the orcas only from the shore. They had also kayaked among them. One of the things Dylan loved most about living here was being out in the kayak and watching as the whales worked as a team to capture fish. He was going to miss this pod as much as anything else when they returned to the city.

"The orcas don't seem to mind the rough seas," his father said.

They watched as the pod swam, dorsal fins appearing and disappearing under the waves, until it vanished around the point and was gone. Then the boat appeared.

Chapter Two

While the orcas had glided through the waves, the boat looked as if it was caught in a battle. It was bouncing on the waves and getting tossed by the wind. It wasn't a big boat—less than sixty feet—and it looked much smaller today, swallowed up by the waves.

"There he is!" Dylan yelled.

On the bow of the boat, in a bright-yellow rain slicker, stood his grandpa.

He waved at them, and Dylan waved back.

The boat edged closer and closer. The first mate, Mr. Singh, appeared on the deck. He had a rope in his hands.

"I'll help them dock," Dylan's father said.

As the boat neared the dock, Mr. Singh tossed the rope, and Dylan's father caught it. The boat edged in and then bumped against the big tires that ringed the dock. Mr. Singh jumped off and tied the stern while Dylan's father tied the bow.

Dylan's grandpa got off, and there were hugs and greetings for everybody. Dylan got a particularly big hug from his grandpa.

"Looked pretty rough out there," Dylan's mother said.

"Not as rough as it's going to get," his grandpa said.

"He's right," Mr. Singh said. He placed three large bags—Dylan's grandpa's—on the dock. "Captain Ken said the marine weather report has warned that the winds are going to pick up even more. So the waves are probably going to get bigger."

Dylan bit on his lower lip—something he always did when he was nervous. His grandpa had arrived safely, but his parents were about to leave. They had a show of their paintings and photographs in the city that had been planned for months, and it was very important to them.

Captain Ken Fukushima climbed off the boat, and everyone greeted him. He and Mr. Singh piloted this boat on a regular run through the islands every two or three weeks. Everything Dylan's family needed came on this boat. Big bins of groceries arrived, along with paints and canvases, toys, clothing and whatever was needed to fix things on the property. The cabin was even older than Grandpa, and there was always something going wrong or needing to be fixed.

"We have to leave again as soon as possible," Captain Ken said.

Dylan's father could tell that his son was feeling anxious about the storm.

"We'll be all right," he said to him.

"I've seen it a lot worse than this," his mother agreed.

Dylan didn't look convinced.

"It's rough, but it's nothing we can't handle. We won't let anything happen to your parents," Captain Ken added.

His father bent down and looked
Dylan in the eyes. "We'll be back in
three days. Okay?"

Dylan nodded. "You should go.
Grandpa will take care of me."

"Would you please put our things
aboard?" his mother said to Mr. Singh.

Along with their luggage, they had
four wooden boxes that contained her
latest paintings and her husband's latest

photographs, all of them framed and ready to be displayed.

Grandpa put a hand on Captain Ken's shoulder. "Nobody in the world I trust more than this man."

Captain Ken and Dylan's grandfather had known each other for what seemed like forever. They had both lived on this island when they were little and their fathers worked at the old cannery on the far side. The cannery had been abandoned decades ago and now sat deserted and falling to pieces.

"We'll help you get your bags up to the cabin," Dylan's father said.

"Dylan and I can take of it," Grandpa said. "It's better that you leave sooner than later, right, Ken?"

The captain nodded. "I'd like to try to stay ahead of the main part of the storm."

"We'll get the bags up there without you," Grandpa said.

Dylan's mother looked unsure.

Grandpa read her expression. "Don't worry. I'm better than ever. No pain. I'm practically a bionic man."

Dylan's grandpa had had his hip replaced two months earlier. It was healing well, but it still caused him some discomfort.

"We'll be fine. I have my big, strong grandson to help me."

She wasn't completely convinced, but she knew there was no point arguing with her father. He had always been stubborn and had only gotten more so with age.

Chapter Three

Dylan and his grandpa waved as the boat chugged away. It seemed so little on the big ocean. They stood on the dock and watched until it disappeared around the point.

"We'd better get these bags up before the storm hits," Grandpa said.

"What's in all those bags?"

"My clothes and a few...well... surprises."

"What sort of surprises?" Dylan asked.

"If I told you, they wouldn't be surprises. You'll see. We'll work together to take this first one."

Together they picked up the first bag.

"It's heavy!" Dylan said.

"Some surprises are heavier than others," Grandpa said with a smile.

Dylan's grandpa was famous for doing the unexpected. His daughter claimed he was like a little kid who could afford to buy whatever toys he wanted. And he did. There was no telling what he'd brought with him.

"You've grown so much," Grandpa said.

Dylan shrugged.

"You've done four months' worth of growing since I last saw you."

"You've changed too."

"Have I?"

"You're hardly limping."

"It's so much better. No limp and hardly any pain. Not perfect but better."

The path was steep and rocky, and they carried the bag between them along the trail. The cabin was a long way from the dock. They finally got there and went inside. Grandpa let out a big sigh. "It's good to be home."

"I'm happy you're here."

"So am I." Grandpa gave his grandson another big hug. "Being here takes me back to when I was young. Do you know how long it's been since I was your age?"

"A hundred years?"

His grandpa laughed. "Closer to two hundred."

"Are you going to tell me what you brought with you now?"

"Not yet. One bag up and two to go. We should get moving. The storm isn't waiting."

"We could use my wagon to get the others," Dylan said.

"Smart. Very smart."

Dylan went outside and circled around to the shed where the wagon was kept.

His grandpa looked around the cabin. It did feel good to be back in the home where he had grown up. He'd have time to read and walk the beach and the paths he knew so well, but he also knew there would be lots to do. The cabin was even older than him, and there were always things that needed to be repaired or replaced. Dylan's parents were talented artists, but neither of them was good with tools. They could paint or take a picture of something that needed to be fixed, but they couldn't fix it. It would be up to Grandpa to fix all the things that needed to be fixed.

Dylan returned with the wagon, and together they hurried back to the dock. The sky was getting darker, and the first drops of rain had started to fall. They hoped they'd get the other two bags up before the rain got heavier.

Chapter Four

Dylan and his grandpa sat at the table, eating dinner by candlelight and the light of the fireplace. The storm had gotten worse and worse, the rain pounding down and the winds getting stronger, until finally it had taken out the power. That wasn't unusual, and the cabin had a backup generator. Unfortunately, the backup generator was one of the things Grandpa had to fix—along with a leak in the roof, a back door that wasn't opening properly, a window that wasn't closing and a sink that was clogged.

Dylan's parents had both grown up in a city, where you just called a plumber or a roofer to fix whatever went wrong. Out here there was nobody to help, so you learned to do everything yourself. Grandpa had been given a list of the things he needed to fix. Tomorrow he would radio Dylan's parents and ask them to bring the supplies and parts he needed when they returned to the island. Of course, he could only radio out if the power came back on or if he fixed the generator. No power meant no radio, no cell phones and no internet.

Outside the wind whistled loudly through the trees, and the rain pounded down on the roof. Dylan was happy to be inside, safe and dry and warm. He'd been even happier to hear that his parents had made shore before the storm hit fully. Captain Ken had radioed to tell them. Thank goodness it had been before the power went out, or Dylan would have worried all night.

"I think it's time for your surprises," Grandpa said. "You clear the table, and I'll get the items."

"Items?" Dylan asked excitedly.

"Like, I said, surprises. More than one."

Grandpa went to the bedroom and grabbed the heaviest bag. By the time he returned with it, the table was cleared and Dylan was anxiously waiting. Grandpa put down the bag and opened it without letting Dylan see inside. He pulled out the first item.

"Wow!" Dylan exclaimed.

It was a big, beautiful kite that looked like an eagle. His grandpa put in the supports, and the eagle's wings opened.

"It's life-size. I brought along over five hundred feet of string. We can make it soar. And speaking of soaring..." He reached into the bag and placed the second item on the table.

"It's a drone!" Dylan said excitedly.

It was black with silver trim. It had four little rotors with red blades.

"It has a camera, so we can take pictures and livestream video," Grandpa explained.

Grandpa took out a big controller. "It's remote control. Of course, we're going to have to wait for the storm to pass. It has to be a lot calmer than it is tonight before we can launch it."

Dylan had one more reason to hope it would be calm the next day—so he could play with the drone.

"It can fly for almost thirty minutes at a time. I'm excited that I'm going to be able to see this island in a way I've never seen it before," Grandpa said. "I'm really looking forward to flying it."

"Grandpa, will I be able to fly it too?"

His grandfather laughed. "You're not only going to be flying it—I'm sure you'll be much better at it than I will. Now it's time for one last thing."

Grandpa reached into the bag and pulled out the final item. He set it down on the table with a heavy clunk. It looked heavy. It was large and long and made of metal, and it had a handle like a broom.

"This is going to be perfect for tomorrow," Grandpa said.

Dylan stared. "What is it?"

"It's a metal detector."

Dylan tilted his head to the side. "What does it do?"

"It can find things buried in the sand. There's no telling what might be there. We could find some real treasure."

"Treasure?"

"Over the years lots of ships sank off these islands, and some of them were carrying valuable things. Big storms like this can wash things up onto the shore or uncover things that were buried there already," Grandpa explained.

"Really?"

"Tomorrow will be the perfect time for us to go on a treasure hunt!"

Dylan pictured treasure chests and pirates' gold. Who didn't want to find buried treasure?

Chapter Five

By the next morning the storm had passed. The day was sunny, with almost no wind. Perfect weather for flying a kite or a drone. Dylan would have been happy doing either of those things, but he was *really* excited about flying the drone.

Instead they were walking along the beach, his grandpa moving the metal detector above the sand. Whenever it beeped they'd put it aside and dig, looking for what had caused the reaction. So far their "treasure" was some old nails, a couple of rusty tins from the old cannery and a beer can that wasn't very old at all. The only thing they'd uncovered that was even a little interesting was a brass button that could have come from a sailor's uniform.

"As the tide goes out we'll have more shore to search, so this is only going to get better," Grandpa said.

Dylan was not so sure about *that*— he didn't know how things could get more boring. He had been hoping for gold coins or a pirate sword or, well, something better than a few rusty old nails. Still, every time the detector beeped he couldn't help but hope there was something special buried there.

On the ocean huge Steller sea lions periscoped out of the water. They seemed curious, watching and barking as Dylan and his grandfather moved along the beach. Up ahead a couple of fat sea lions were sunning themselves on the sand. Dylan loved animals, and there were so many to see out here. And not just otters and sea lions and orcas. The island was home to a herd of deer, a couple of black bears and more birds than he could count.

As Dylan and his grandfather approached them, the sea lions moved back into the water.

Dylan cocked his head to the side. "Did you hear that?"

His grandpa looked up from the metal detector. "I heard the barking, and I hear the waves and seagulls,

but I don't hear anything else. My ears are as old as the rest of me."

"I'm not sure, but I think it's the orcas talking."

"They're probably chasing down lunch," Grandpa said.

When the pod was hunting, they talked to each other as they drove the fish into the shallows and surrounded them.

"It's different," Dylan said. "They sound…they sound…upset."

Grandpa put down the metal detector and opened up his bag. He handed Dylan a pair of binoculars. "Go up on the rocks over there and see if you can spot them."

Dylan grabbed the binoculars and ran toward the rocks where the beach dead-ended. They were steep and big and jutted well out into the ocean. He wanted to move fast, but he had to move carefully.

The rocks were sharp, and they were wet, which made them slick.

Dylan knew his parents wouldn't have let him climb up here by himself. They always wanted to be there, holding his hand every step of the way, but his grandpa was different. He always let Dylan do things that would have made his parents nervous.

Dylan slipped a little, almost falling onto his hands. He thought that maybe, for a couple of those steps, a helping hand would have been nice.

He finally got to the top of the outcrop. High up here he could see much more. He looked out on the ocean. The surface was so calm and flat that he instantly picked out the dorsal fins and backs of the orcas. They were so close there was no need for the binoculars.

"Do you see them?" Grandpa yelled up from the beach below.

"Yes!" Dylan tried to count the fins he could see. It was hard because the whales were circling and going under and coming up. Up here, closer to them, he could hear their calls more clearly. They were making many sounds, and it did seem like they were upset. But why? What were they upset about?

The whales kept swimming in circles just a short distance from shore. Dylan wished they'd go farther away from the sharp rocks. Dorsal fins kept coming up out of the water and going back under the waves. It looked like the whole pod was here. Wait—where was Oreo? He was little, so he couldn't stay underwater as long as the other orcas could, but he was also harder to spot among the others and the waves. And then Dylan saw him. Oreo was on the rocks at the bottom of the outcrop.

It had taken Grandpa some time to scale the rocks. He and Dylan stood there, looking down at the ocean and the little orca stranded on the rocks. He was no more than fifteen feet below them. Out in the water the pod was still circling and calling. It sounded

like crying. Now Dylan knew why they were so upset.

"How did this happen?" Dylan asked.

"There could be lots of reasons. It might just be that the bottom of the ocean was changed by the storm. Maybe they were chasing salmon and then the tide went out and he got trapped. That can happen to the younger orcas because they're not as experienced."

"But he's going to be all right, isn't he?"

His grandpa didn't answer right away.

"Grandpa, he'll be okay, right?"

His grandpa shook his head. "I don't know."

"We have to do something to help," Dylan pleaded.

"I'm not sure if there's much we can do."

"We have to get him back into the water."

"I don't see how we can do that. He's too big for us to move. Besides, it's going to get harder. The tide is still going out."

Dylan hadn't thought of that. The little whale was already out of the water, and it was only going to get worse.

"We have to call somebody! My parents...or the coast guard...or I don't know."

"Remember, the radio still isn't working, but even if we could call for help, there's nobody who can get here in time. We're the only two people on the island right now."

"Then we have to do something."

"The only help is hours away. We have to hope the water rises enough at high tide to allow the whale to float back out, but that's still at least eight hours away."

"Then Oreo will be okay in eight hours."

Grandpa shook his head. "I don't think he can live that long out of the water."

"But why not? He's a mammal, so he breathes air," Dylan said.

"He breathes air, but he still needs the water. Without water his skin will dry out. Without water to provide protection, he'll get sunburned and dehydrated. The only way we could stop those things is…well…"

"What? What could we do?" Dylan asked.

"We'd have to drape something over Oreo to protect him from the sun. And keep him wet. To stop his skin from drying out. But we can't do that from up here, and, to be honest, I don't think I can get down to those rocks."

"I can," Dylan said.

"I can't let you do that by yourself," Grandpa said. "It's too dangerous."

"What if you made it safer?" Dylan asked.

"How would I do that?"

"I don't know, but you can figure it out. I know you can."

His grandpa didn't answer. He looked like he was thinking. And then he smiled. And Dylan knew he had an idea.

Chapter Six

Dylan was wearing thick rubber boots and gloves and a bright-orange life jacket. Attached to the life jacket was a yellow rope. Grandpa had tied the other end of the rope around one of the rocks. They had all the gear they'd need. It had taken them half a dozen trips to get everything in place.

Dylan looked over the edge of the cliff. Below him, no more than thirty feet away and fifteen feet down, Oreo lay on the rocks. The receding tide had left the orca and the rocks he was trapped on even farther from the water.

Even from this distance Dylan could see that the little orca was hurt. There were slashes of red visible on his tail fin. He'd been cut. Dylan wondered how much worse it might be in the places he couldn't see—like Oreo's belly, which was pressed against the sharp rocks.

"Are you sure you want to do this?" Grandpa asked.

"We have no choice."

"We could wait until the tide goes all the way out and then climb up to him from the beach."

"You said that wouldn't be for another hour. Can he...can he...can he live another hour?"

"All I know is the sooner he gets helped, the better. The sun is starting to shine on the cliff and soon it will be directly on him," Grandpa said.

"Then I should go now."

"I'll lower you down, and remember I'm right here if you need me."

Dylan knew.

"Stay off to the side of his body and away from his mouth."

"Orcas don't hurt people," Dylan said.

"No telling what a scared, trapped animal will do."

Dylan nodded. Learning about the animals of the island was part of his homeschooling this year. He'd learned about bears, deer, eagles and sea lions, but orcas were his favorite.

He knew that orcas lived in families and cared for each other. That they were smart and communicated with sounds. That some pods—like this one—ate fish, and other pods ate seals and other whales and dolphins. He knew there had never been a person killed by an orca in the wild. But he also knew they had between forty and fifty-six very large and very sharp teeth in a powerful jaw. And he knew that if he was scared, Oreo must be terrified.

"We have an audience," Grandpa said.

"We do?" Dylan asked hopefully.

Grandpa gestured toward the open ocean. For an instant Dylan thought he meant other people. There was no boat, but three members of the pod were "standing," extending their heads far out of the water. He'd been focusing so much on Oreo that he'd temporarily forgotten about the pod circling just beyond the rocks.

"Do they know we're trying to help?" Dylan asked.

"They're pretty smart, so I hope so."

At that instant Oreo cried out, and the pod started calling to him. A series of high-pitched sounds went back and forth. Dylan hoped they were telling Oreo that help was coming.

Dylan started down the rocks. The loose end of the rope trailed behind him, Grandpa holding the other end tightly in case Dylan slipped. At a birthday party the previous year on the mainland, Dylan had done some rock climbing in a special gym. This was different. Here the rocks were wet and slick. And sharp. Carefully he found places to put his feet and places to hold with his hands. He knew he had to go slowly. A few more steps down, and he was there.

Oreo rotated his eye so that he was looking up at Dylan. Dylan could see the fear in his eyes. Did Oreo see the fear in his? He had never been so close to an animal this big. Oreo was just a young orca, but he was much bigger than Dylan.

"It's going to be okay. I'm coming to save you," Dylan said.

Saying those words made him feel better, even if Oreo couldn't understand them.

"Here come the sheets!" Grandpa yelled.

Grandpa lowered a blue bucket. It slowly bumped down the rocks until it was low enough that Dylan could

reach out and grab it. He placed the bucket beside him and pulled out the first sheet. It was blue and green and from his parents' bed. It had been soaked in seawater and was heavy and awkward to unfold. Dylan could see blood from one of the cuts near Oreo's tail. He started to spread the sheet, and Oreo cried out. Dylan stopped. He was shocked. Oreo began shaking, and he moved his tail up and down. He opened his mouth, and those white, sharp teeth practically glowed. Was this hurting the little orca? Dylan didn't know what to do. He just froze in place.

"You have to keep going!" Grandpa called.

"But I think it's hurting him."

"You're not hurting him. He's just scared. Besides, if you don't cover him, he'll be a lot worse off. Spread the sheet."

Dylan hoped his grandpa was right —but even if he wasn't, what choice did Dylan have? He started to spread the sheet again, and this time when Oreo cried out, Dylan didn't stop. He covered up the tail and then pulled the sheet over Oreo's back and up toward the dorsal fin. As he'd covered the tail, he'd seen blood from one of the cuts being absorbed by the sheet.

"It's okay," Dylan explained to Oreo. "I'm doing this to protect you from the sun. I'm here to help you—it's going to be all right."

Dylan took a second sheet and draped it over the dorsal fin, tapping it down so that it was pressed against the skin.

The little orca reacted again but not as badly. Dylan took out a third sheet, being careful not to cover the breathing hole on Oreo's back and keeping the sheet away the orca's mouth.

The bucket was now empty. But it wouldn't be for long. There was water pooled in the rocks just below them. He dipped the bucket, filled it with water and pulled it up. He poured the water onto the whale. It showered down Oreo's dorsal fin and onto his back and sides.

"Does that feel better?" Dylan asked Oreo.

Oreo answered by opening and closing his mouth.

"That's perfect!" Grandpa yelled. "Keep going!"

Bucket by bucket, Dylan poured water from the little pool onto the whale.

He knew this was keeping Oreo's skin moist, cooling it down and keeping the sheets wet so they'd stick to and protect the skin. All he had to do was keep doing this. For the next six or seven hours.

Chapter Seven

Dylan had stripped off layers of clothing as the day went on and the sun got hotter. But he kept his life jacket on. It and the rope tied to it kept him safe. His arms were tired. His whole body was tired. It had been over two hours of hard work. He wanted to stop, but he knew he couldn't. Oreo needed him.

Over time, as Dylan collected and poured water, the little orca became calmer and calmer.

"See, Oreo? I told you I was going to help you."

Dylan was glad the orca wasn't so upset. Oreo was quiet now. That was good. Wait. *Was* it? Was Oreo calm, or was he...was he...? Then Dylan heard Oreo breathing, exhaling through his blowhole, and Dylan felt like he could breathe again too.

"Take the hose!" Grandpa yelled.

His grandpa was now standing on the beach. The water had receded enough that he was able to stand there below the rocks. Dylan reached down and grabbed the end of the hose his grandpa had held up to him.

The other end of the hose was attached by duct tape to a bicycle air pump.

"Let's hope for the best," Grandpa said.

He waded into the water and started to pump the handle. It was supposed to send up ocean water…but at first there was nothing. It wasn't working! But then water started coming out.

"It's working!" Dylan screamed. He sprayed water along the whole length of Oreo's body. This hose gave him much more water than the bucket had, and it was so much easier!

After a few minutes Grandpa stopped pumping. The pump had done the work of dozens and dozens of buckets of water.

Dylan was hungry. All his hard work—and excitement—had given him an appetite. His grandpa had passed some food down to him earlier—he'd eaten apples and a sandwich and some granola bars. It was time for another apple.

He sat down, his back against a rock and right beside Oreo's head. The whale followed Dylan's movement with his one eye. Oreo still looked unsure, but he was calm.

"I wish I could share this apple with you," Dylan said to Oreo. "But you'll have to wait until you get back in the water. You know you're going back into the water, right?"

The whale was silent, but his tail rose ever so slightly.

"In a few hours you'll be able to use that tail again. Just lay still now. Don't move around."

The pod members called from the deep water. The outgoing tide had forced them farther away. Oreo replied to the calls. Both sides of the conversation seemed calmer. Maybe they all understood that Dylan was there to help.

"We're friends now," he said. "The next time I'm out in my kayak, you better come up and say hello." He smiled. "You can even splash me a little bit to make up for me splashing you."

Again Oreo raised his tail and then slightly opened his mouth.

Did he just smile at me?

Dylan finished his apple and then stood up and looked down at the beach.

"How much longer?" he yelled.

"The tide is starting to come back in. I'm going to have to move in an hour or so. I think it'll still be about four hours before the water gets up to your level. Are you going to be all right?"

"I'd be all right even if it was another forty hours."

"I knew you would be! I'm going to start pumping again in a few minutes."

Dylan stared at the back of the whale and adjusted the sheets, making sure there was no skin exposed to the sun. The sun was right above them now, and it was bright. It was hot and getting hotter. He made sure Oreo's blowhole was free. Then he placed his hand on the white patch by Oreo's eye. The orca's skin was wet and cool. So much cooler than it had been when all of this had started. Despite the rising temperature and the sun getting higher in the sky, he was managing to keep Oreo cool.

Dylan looked directly at one of Oreo's eyes, which was looking up at him. Dylan was amazed at how small the eye was compared to the size of the whale. It wasn't that much bigger or different than Dylan's—just darker.

And then he realized they had something else in common. He could see that the whale was thinking. Maybe about Dylan or about the situation or about his pod. But he was thinking. And more than that. The fear was gone, and Dylan thought he saw hope in the eye looking back at him.

Chapter Eight

Minute by minute, inch by inch, the tide kept coming in. The rising water was just below Oreo and Dylan now, and the waves crashed up and over them. They were both soaked. Those waves were doing the work that Dylan had been doing with the bucket and the hose.

"It's time to take off the sheets," his grandpa yelled down. He was back at the top of the outcrop.

With the sun behind the rocks now and the waves spraying up, the sheets weren't needed anymore. And they had to be removed in case somehow they got tangled around Oreo's tail or fins and kept him trapped him on the rocks even when the water got high enough for him to swim away.

Dylan pulled away the sheet at Oreo's tail. It was streaked with blood. He didn't think his parents would ever use it on their bed again. For a split second he thought they might be mad at him for ruining it, but he knew they'd understand. In response to the sheet being removed, Oreo lifted his tail high into the air.

Gently Dylan ran his hand over the skin near Oreo's tail. It was cool and smooth and rubbery to the touch.

The cuts weren't bleeding anymore. Dylan bundled up the sheet and dropped it into the blue bucket. He removed the second sheet and felt Oreo's back. The skin was smooth and cool here as well. He dropped the second sheet into the bucket. That left just the one covering the orca's upper back and head.

"It's almost over," he said to Oreo as he pulled the sheet away. The whale followed him with one dark eye.

Dylan put the sheet in the bucket and signaled for his grandpa to pull it up. The blue bucket bounced up the side of the rocky outcrop.

Dylan knew there was really nothing left for him to do now, but he didn't want to leave. He got the feeling that Oreo didn't want him to leave either.

At least Oreo wasn't as alone as he had been. With the rising water, the rest of the pod had moved closer. They kept calling out to Oreo. He answered back, but his voice was quiet. Was he too exhausted to respond?

A big wave broke directly over them, and as it washed away Dylan felt himself being pulled outward. The wave was so strong that it even rocked Oreo slightly. It was definitely time to leave.

Dylan worked his way up to Oreo's head and bent down so he could look directly into the whale's one big black eye.

"I've got to go now," he said. "You're going soon too. I'm going back to my grandpa, and you're going back to your family."

Of course, Oreo didn't answer, but Dylan was sure he understood.

"I've done everything I could. I hope you know that." Dylan straightened. "I'm coming up!" he called to his grandpa.

Grandpa gave him a little wave and then gathered in the slack on the rope. He'd help Dylan climb by pulling in the rope and keeping it taut.

Dylan reached up and found a hold on the rock. His hands were stiff and numb, and the soaking-wet gloves weren't helping. He felt so tired. He'd been down here with Oreo for almost ten hours. Would he be able to climb up the rocks? He had no choice.

Carefully he moved upward. With each foot he climbed, his grandpa reeled in the rope, helping him. Dylan focused on each step, making sure his feet were in a solid place and his hands had a good grip. Just a few more feet and he'd be at the top, and—his foot slipped and he fell against the rock, smacking his knees. He was more scared than hurt as he scrambled to regain his footing. Thank goodness the rope was there to hold me in place, he thought.

"You're almost here," Grandpa said. He offered Dylan a hand and pulled him to the top.

Dylan turned to look back down at where he'd spent the last ten hours beside Oreo. Even bigger waves were splashing up and over the rocks, showering down on the orca's back. The ocean was now doing what Dylan had been doing for hours. And it still had to do what he and his grandpa couldn't—free Oreo from the rocks.

The water was rising quickly as the tide rushed in. High tide was less than thirty minutes away. The water seemed to be rising faster by the second. It wouldn't be too much longer before it would free Oreo.

"He's going to be able to go soon, right?" Dylan asked.

"I hope that's what happens."

"But...but why wouldn't it?"

"I just want you to be prepared."

"Prepared for what?"

Grandpa didn't answer at first. Just like he could tell when Oreo was thinking, Dylan could tell that his grandpa was thinking now too.

"Oreo has been out of the water for a long time," Grandpa began.

"But we kept him wet and cool and covered so he wouldn't get sunburned. We did everything you said we needed to do."

"We did—*you* did—everything that could be done. But we couldn't keep his own weight off him."

"I don't understand."

"Whales are meant to float, not lie down. His weight has been pressing down on those rocks, and this could have damaged his heart or lungs."

"He was breathing okay. I could hear him breathing the whole time I was down there."

"There could still be damage. And I worry about the cuts. He might be more hurt than we can see," Grandpa said.

"I didn't see any blood coming from underneath," Dylan said.

"That doesn't mean he wasn't scraped up when he got on the rocks or that he won't be cut trying to get off the rocks too soon. He has to wait for the water to get high enough for him to float and to swim free."

Dylan hadn't thought of that. If only he could tell Oreo to wait.

At that moment the pod members started talking. It sounded like it was all of them. They were loud, and Oreo started to answer back. Were they telling him to wait or asking him to come back? If only Dylan knew. If only he could speak to Oreo and tell him to wait. But he was helpless.

"Not yet," his grandpa said quietly. "Just stay there a little bit longer."

Oreo started to move more. He wiggled around. He lifted and lowered his tail, and water splashed up into the air.

"Just a little bit longer," Dylan said. "Hang in there and—"

A giant wave crashed up onto the rocks, throwing spray so high that it hit Dylan and his grandpa. Below, it hit Oreo hard, rocking him sideways. He was close to floating! Then another wave hit, and a third and a fourth, and then Oreo popped forward! He was off the rocks and in the water!

"Look at him go!" Grandpa yelled.

Oreo raced out into open water.

"He's all right!" Dylan exclaimed.

"Judging by how fast he's moving, he's better than all right!"

Oreo was soon surrounded by the rest of the pod. They swam all around him for a minute and then started to head out, away from the shore and the rocks. Dylan and his grandpa watched as different dorsal fins surfaced and disappeared. Oreo's appeared among those of the bigger whales—his family. Dylan and Grandpa stood atop the rocks and watched until the pod disappeared.

"We did it," Dylan said.

"Mostly you did it. Funny, we came down to the beach to try to find some treasure, and I think we did."

"But it was only treasure when we set it free."

Chapter Nine

Dylan sat on the end of the dock. His parents and Grandpa stood behind him. The pod had returned! The orcas had pushed a school of fish into the cove and were feeding. They had worked as a team, fencing in and then eating the fish. Dorsal fins broke the surface continually. The whole pod was here—including Oreo! His little triangular dorsal fin continually broke the surface.

"It's always amazing to see them feed," Grandpa said. He was watching through the binoculars.

Dylan's father had set up his best camera with its biggest lens. He was snapping photographs, although he kept muttering that "pictures couldn't capture it."

It was all very exciting, but Dylan was interested in only one orca—Oreo. It was wonderful to see him out there!

It had been three days since his parents returned to the island and five since he'd helped the little orca off the rocks. Every day since the rescue he'd gone to the dock and stared out at the ocean, hoping to catch a glimpse of Oreo so he'd know he was all right. Twice his parents had taken him out sea kayaking, thinking if they were farther out, they had a better chance of seeing the pod. It hadn't worked. Dylan and his grandpa had sent the drone out over the open water every day to try to catch a glimpse of the whales, but that hadn't worked either. Dylan had loved flying the drone, but what he really wanted was to see the whales—and it was finally happening.

"I guess there's no question that he's fine," Grandpa said, putting down the binoculars.

"Thanks to Dylan," his mother said.

"It wasn't just me," Dylan said. "It was me and Grandpa."

"It wasn't me down there on the rocks. I helped, but you did the work."

Dylan's mother reached down and gave her son a little squeeze on the shoulder. "We're all so proud of you," she said.

They'd told him that at least a dozen times.

What they hadn't said was how they were also grateful that he hadn't been hurt helping the whale. What he'd done was dangerous.

"I wish Oreo would come a little closer," Dylan said.

"He's probably not going to stray too far from his mother," Grandpa said.

"Or come too close to shore for a long time," his mother added.

"I guess you're right. Still, it would be nice," Dylan said.

"Just be happy he's here," Grandpa said. "Watching those orcas feed has worked up my appetite."

"Supper will be ready in a few minutes," Dylan's father said. His parents took turns cooking, and tonight was his father's. Their meal was bubbling away in a slow cooker. "Why don't we go to the cabin, wash up and—"

"Can I stay here a little bit longer?" Dylan asked. "Please?"

"You can stay as long as you want. Come on up to eat when you're ready."

"Here, you might need these," Grandpa said as he handed Dylan the binoculars.

His parents and Grandpa walked down the dock and onto the path, leaving Dylan alone with the pod.

Dylan already knew the whales wouldn't be there much longer. The pod was moving away. It was almost at the entrance to the cove now and would probably head back out to the open ocean soon.

Dylan wanted one more glimpse of Oreo. He brought up the binoculars and scanned the water, looking for one little dorsal fin among the bigger fins and the bigger waves. He couldn't see him. Was he already out of the cove?

Then he heard a whale calling, and it was close. He lowered the binoculars. There, right in front of him, no more than a dozen feet from the end of the dock, was Oreo. He was periscoping out of the water, looking directly at Dylan. Oreo gave a high-pitched call.

"I'm glad to see you and to know you're fine!"

Oreo rose slightly higher out of the water, opened and closed his mouth and then slid down and under the waves. A few seconds later his dorsal fin broke the surface and disappeared again.

Dylan watched as Oreo headed for the entrance of the cove, back to his pod. He watched until Oreo joined his pod and they disappeared into the open ocean.

Dylan stood up. It was time for supper. He was hungry. But more important, he was happy. It was time for Oreo to be with his family and Dylan to be with his.

Nathan looked up from his meal and out the window. There was something pressed against the screen of the door. It was pinned there, moving as the wind blew it back and forth, back and forth. He thought it was very strange how it was moving. Was it a black plastic bag or a piece of paper or…no, it was furry, and it had a tail, and—

"It's a squirrel!" Nathan yelled as he jumped up from the table.

He ran across the kitchen. His father and mother were right behind him. He skidded to a stop at the thin screen door standing between him and the squirrel. His parents stood beside him.

"It's just a baby," his mother said.

Instead of running away, the little squirrel continued to cling to the screen. It tilted its head to the side and looked in at them as they looked out at it.

"He's so cute," Nathan said.

"He *is* cute, but what's he doing here?" his mother asked.

"Maybe he wants to come in and join us for supper," his father joked.

"Could he?" Nathan asked. "I'd share my salad with him."

"He should go back and join *his* family for dinner," Nathan's mother said.

She looked at her husband, and he nodded in agreement.

"Time to go home, little guy," his father said as he gently tapped one of his fingers against the screen.

Instead of running off, the squirrel climbed up the screen until it was at the spot where he'd been tapping. His father moved his finger and tapped at another spot on the screen, and the little animal followed after his finger.

"So what do we do now?" Nathan asked.

"We could close the door, and he might go away," his father suggested.

"That would be rude," Nathan said.

"But it's not like we can bring him in."

Nathan leaned in a little closer to the squirrel. "He's crying."

"I don't think squirrels cry," his mother said. "But I do hear something… it's squeaking."

"He's probably calling for his mother to come and get him," Nathan said.

Nathan's father went to close the door and hesitated. He knew Nathan was concerned. "It'll be okay, Nathan. I'm sure his mother will come and get him as soon as we close the door."

Nathan wanted to believe his father, but he was worried. He nodded his head ever so slightly in agreement.

His father slowly started to close the door and—

"Wait!" Nathan called out. "Look!"

His father stopped. He hoped he'd see the mother squirrel. Instead, he saw what his son had seen.

"It's Batcat," Nathan said.

Eric Walters, Member of the Order of Canada, began writing as a way to get his fifth-grade students interested in reading and writing. He has since published more than 100 novels and picture books. He is a tireless presenter, speaking to over 100,000 students per year in schools across the country. He lives in Guelph, Ontario.